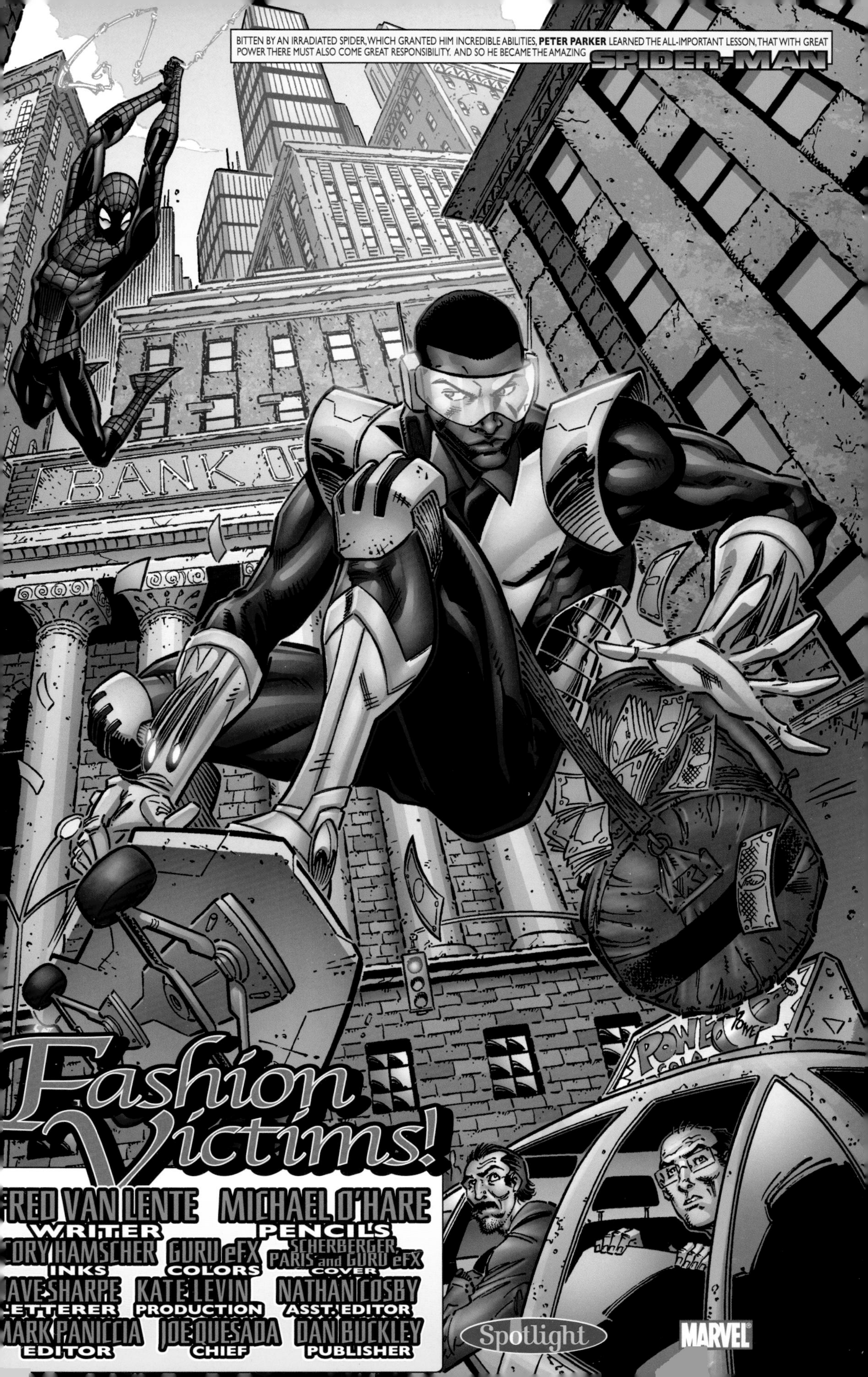
BITTEN BY AN IRRADIATED SPIDER, WHICH GRANTED HIM INCREDIBLE ABILITIES, PETER PARKER LEARNED THE ALL-IMPORTANT LESSON, THAT WITH GREAT POWER THERE MUST ALSO COME GREAT RESPONSIBILITY. AND SO HE BECAME THE AMAZING SPIDER-MAN
BANK OF
Fashion Victims!
FRED VAN LENTE WRITER
MICHAEL O'HARE PENCILS
CORY HAMSCHER INKS
GURU eFX COLORS
SCHERBERGER, PARIS and GURU eFX COVER
DAVE SHARPE LETTERER
KATE LEVIN PRODUCTION
NATHAN COSBY ASST. EDITOR
MARK PANICCIA EDITOR
JOE QUESADA CHIEF
DAN BUCKLEY PUBLISHER
Spotlight
MARVEL

VISIT US AT
www.abdopublishing.com

Reinforced library bound edition published in 2008 by Spotlight, a division of the ABDO Publishing Group, 8000 West 78th Street, Edina, Minnesota 55439. Spotlight produces high-quality reinforced library bound editions for schools and libraries. Published by agreement with Marvel Characters, Inc.

Library of Congress Cataloging-in-Publication Data

Van Lente, Fred.
  Fashion victims! / Fred Van Lente, writer ; Michael O'Hare, pencils ; Cory Hamscher, inks ; GURU eFX, colors ; Scherberger, Paris and GURU eFX, cover ; Dave Sharpe, letterer. -- Reinforced library bound ed.
      p. cm. -- (Spider-man)
  "Marvel age"--Cover.
  Revision of issue 21 of Marvel adventures Spider-man.
  ISBN 978-1-59961-395-6
  1. Graphic novels. I. O'Hare, Michael (Michael S.) II. Marvel adventures. Spider-man. 21. III. Title.

PN6728.S6V36 2008
741.5'973--dc22

                                                                2007020239

All Spotlight books have reinforced library bindings and are manufactured in the United States of America.

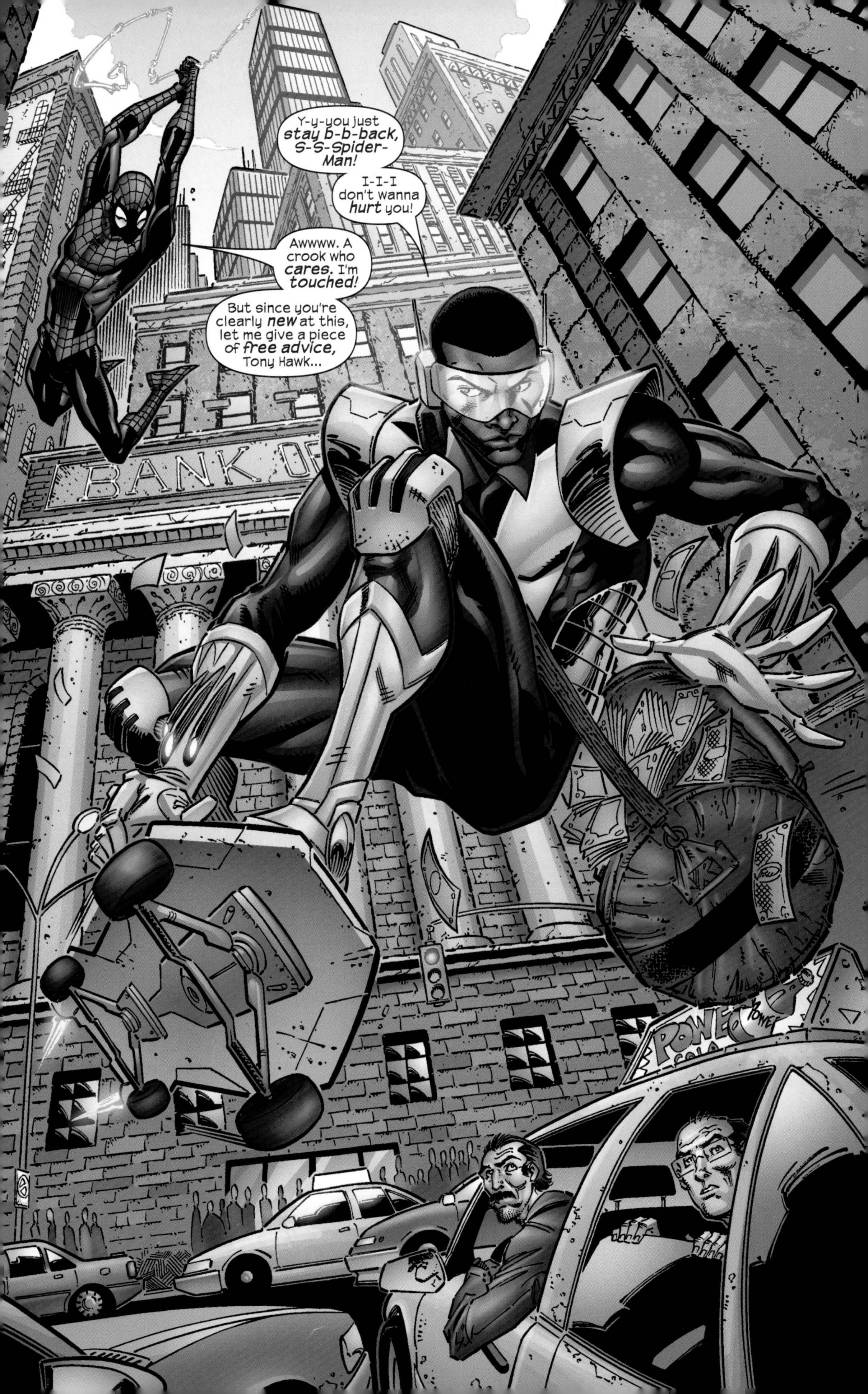
Y-y-you just stay b-b-back, S-S-Spider-Man!
I-I-I don't wanna hurt you!
Awwww. A crook who cares. I'm touched!
But since you're clearly new at this, let me give a piece of free advice, Tony Hawk...
BANK OF

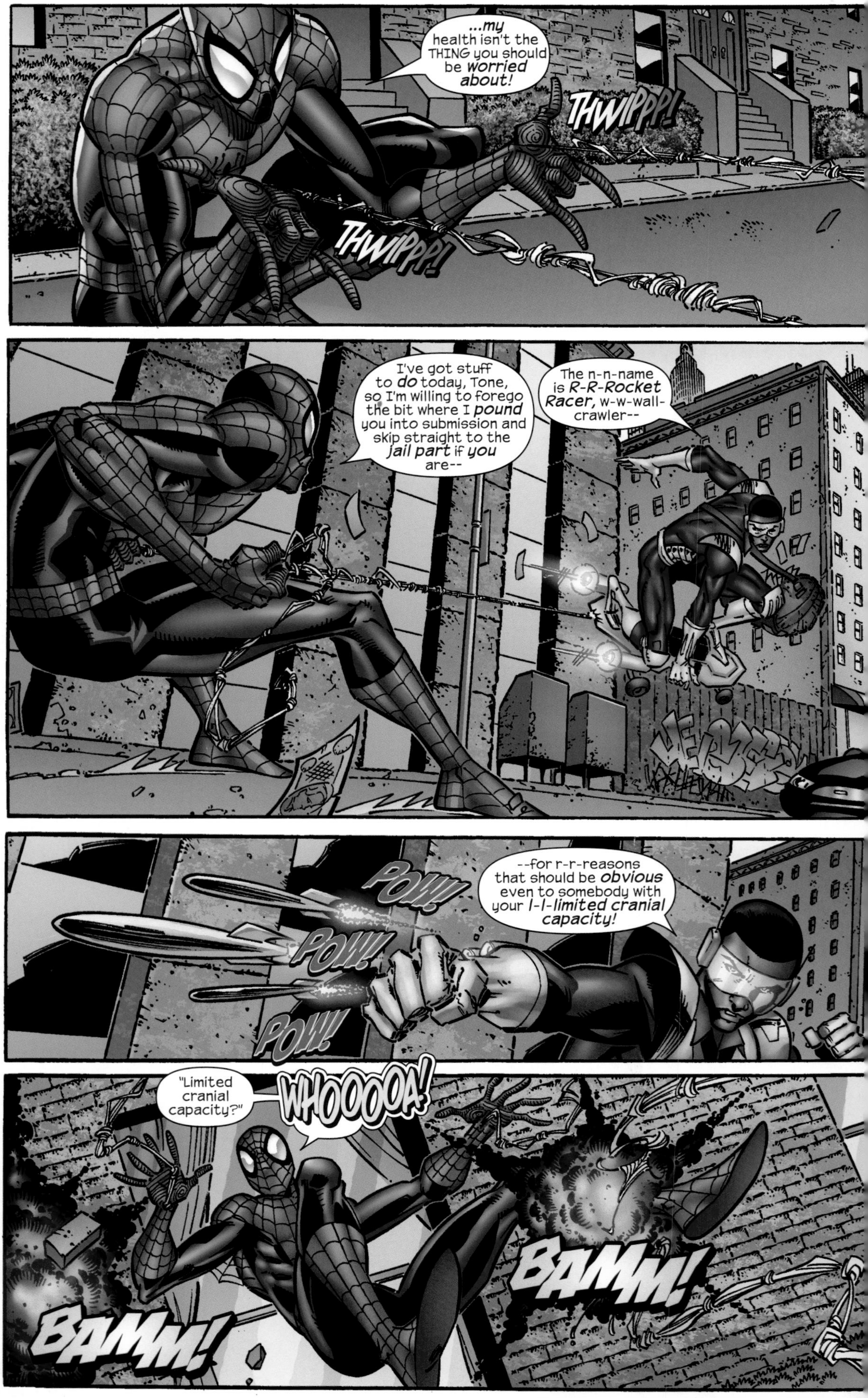
...my health isn't the THING you should be worried about!
THWIPPP!
THWIPPP!
I've got stuff to do today, Tone, so I'm willing to forego the bit where I pound you into submission and skip straight to the jail part if you are--
The n-n-name is R-R-Rocket Racer, w-w-wall-crawler--
--for r-r-reasons that should be obvious even to somebody with your l-l-limited cranial capacity!
POW!!
POW!
POW!
"Limited cranial capacity?"
WHOOOOA!
BAMM!
BAMM!

CRASH!

Well, lookee here!

You sure got a lotta *muscles* on you for a *little guy!*

Ohhhh... Aunt May?

at's is?

One of Rocket Raccoon's *mini-missiles* must have been a *dud!*

Huh! Some kind of *maker's mark.* Must be a *clue...*

...though to *what* I haven't got a...

...uh, clue.

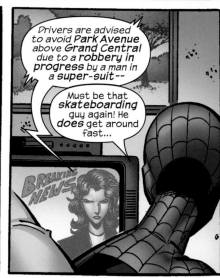

Drivers are advised to avoid *Park Avenue* above *Grand Central* due to a *robbery in progress* by a man in a *super-suit--*

Must be that *skateboarding* guy again! He *does* get around fast...

BREAKING NEWS

Sure you won't stick *around,* squirt? I'd love for you to show me what's under that *mask--*

≈Gulp!≈ *No thanks,* lady!

I'm afraid you'd show me what's under *yours!*

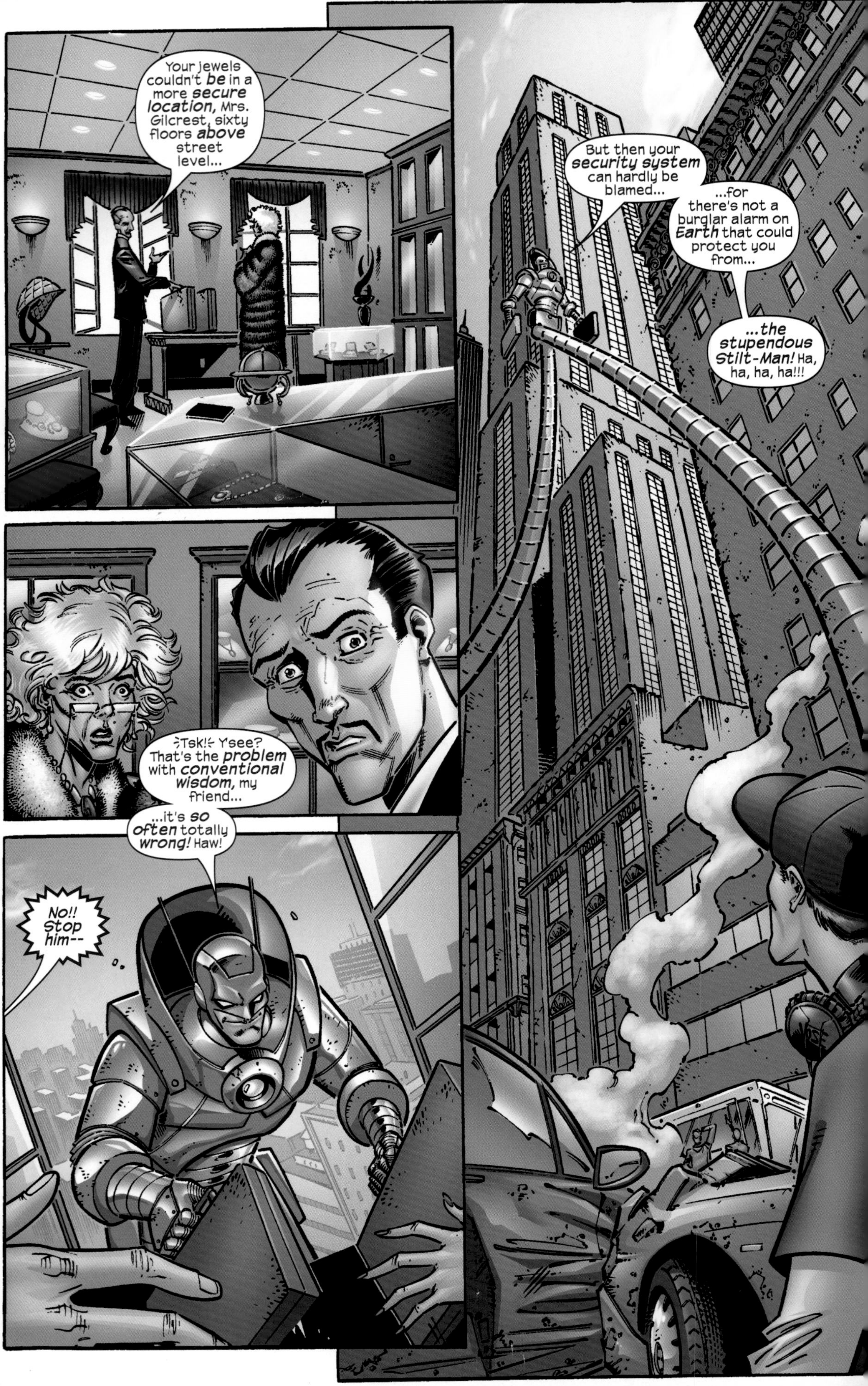
Your jewels couldn't be in a more secure location, Mrs. Gilcrest, sixty floors above street level...
But then your security system can hardly be blamed...
...for there's not a burglar alarm on Earth that could protect you from...
...the stupendous Stilt-Man! Ha, ha, ha, ha!!!
Tsk!! Y'see? That's the problem with conventional wisdom, my friend...
...it's so often totally wrong! Haw!
No!! Stop him--

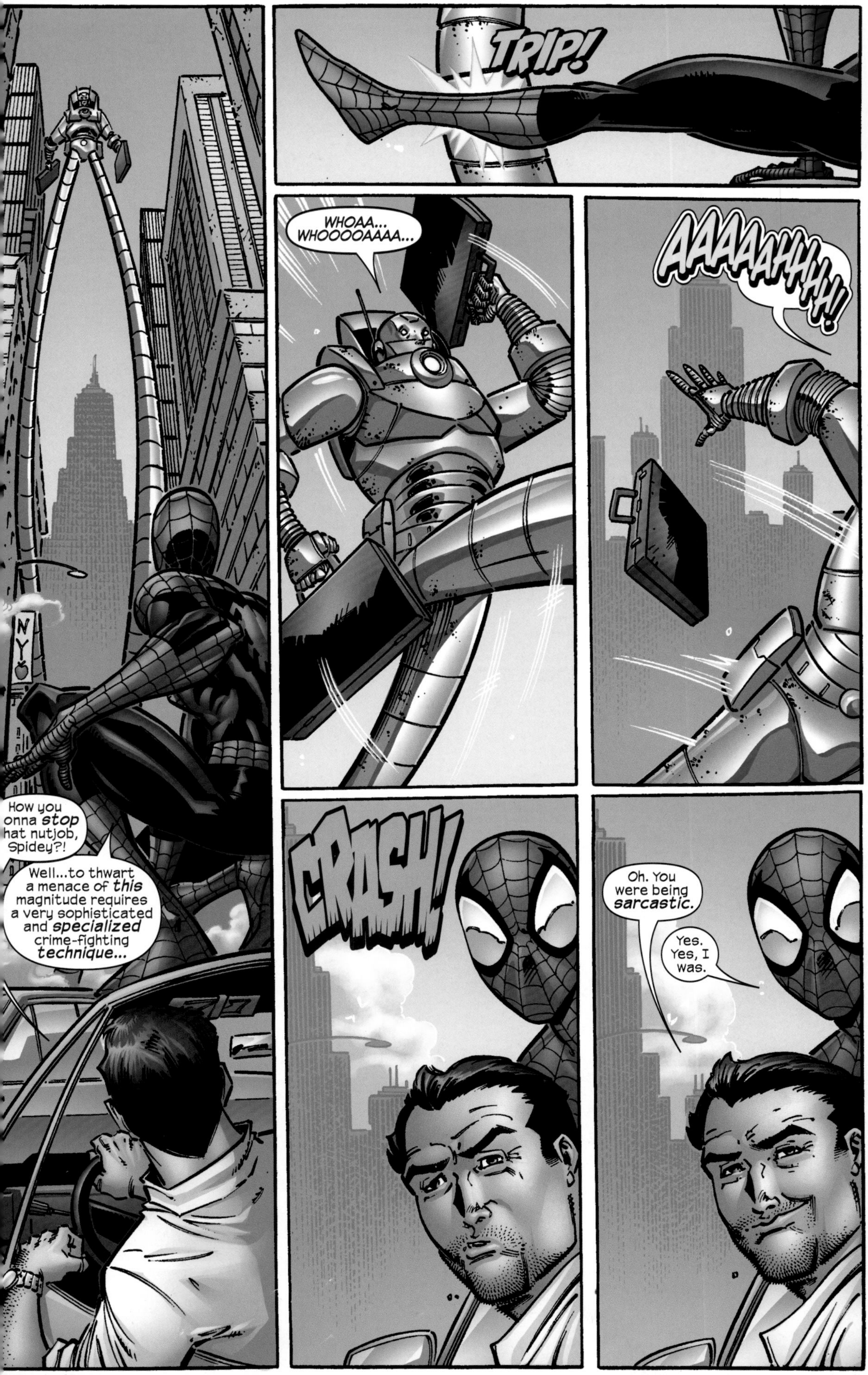
TRIP!
WHOAA... WHOOOOAAAA...
AAAAAHHHH!
How you onna stop hat nutjob, Spidey?!
Well...to thwart a menace of this magnitude requires a very sophisticated and specialized crime-fighting technique...
CRASH!
Oh. You were being sarcastic.
Yes. Yes, I was.

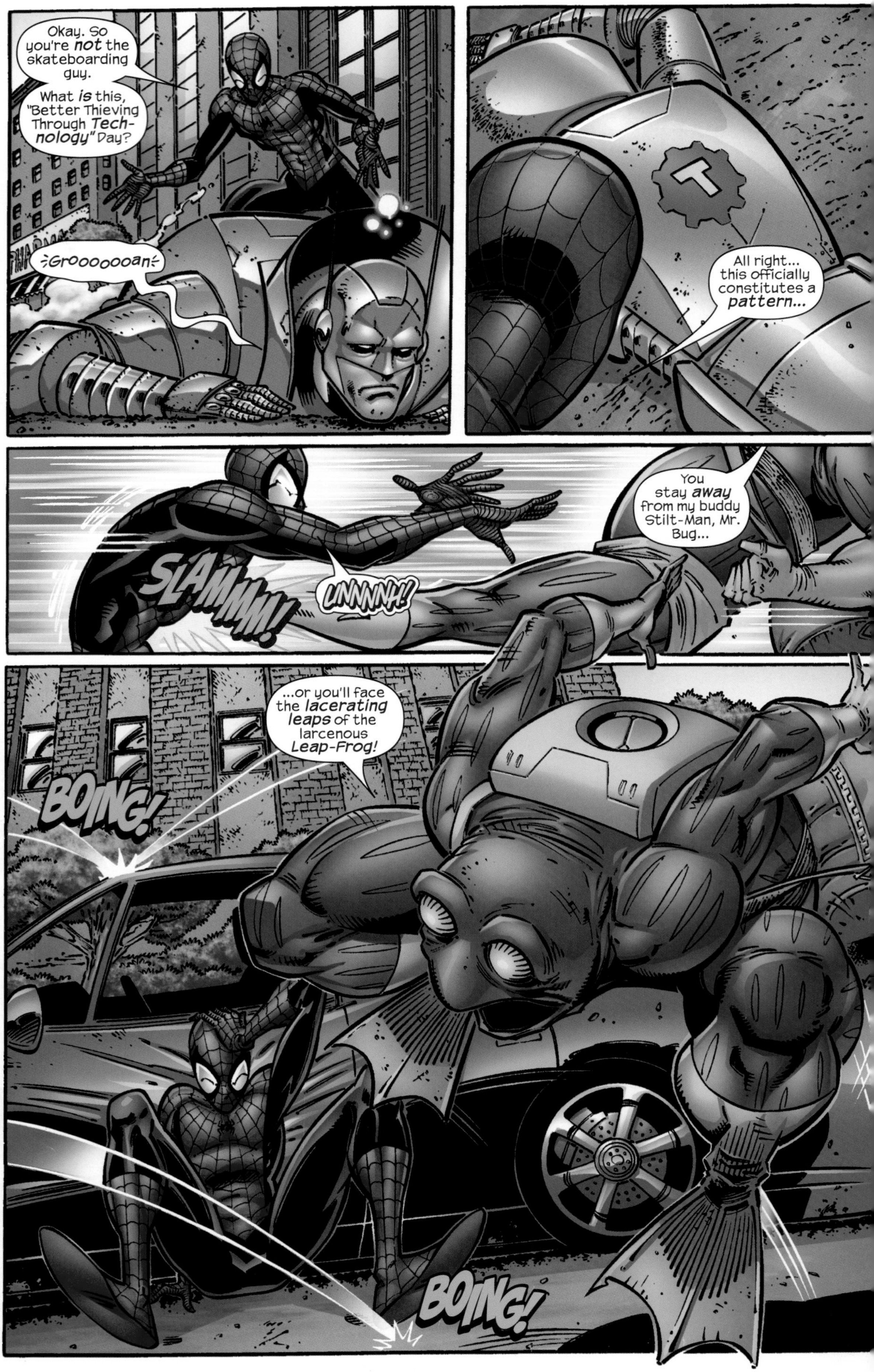
Okay. So you're *not* the skateboarding guy.
What *is* this, "Better Thieving Through *Tech-nology*" Day?
Groooooooan
All right... this officially constitutes a *pattern...*
You stay *away* from my buddy Stilt-Man, Mr. Bug...
SLAMMM!
UNNNNH!
...or you'll face the *lacerating leaps* of the larcenous *Leap-Frog!*
BOING!
BOING!

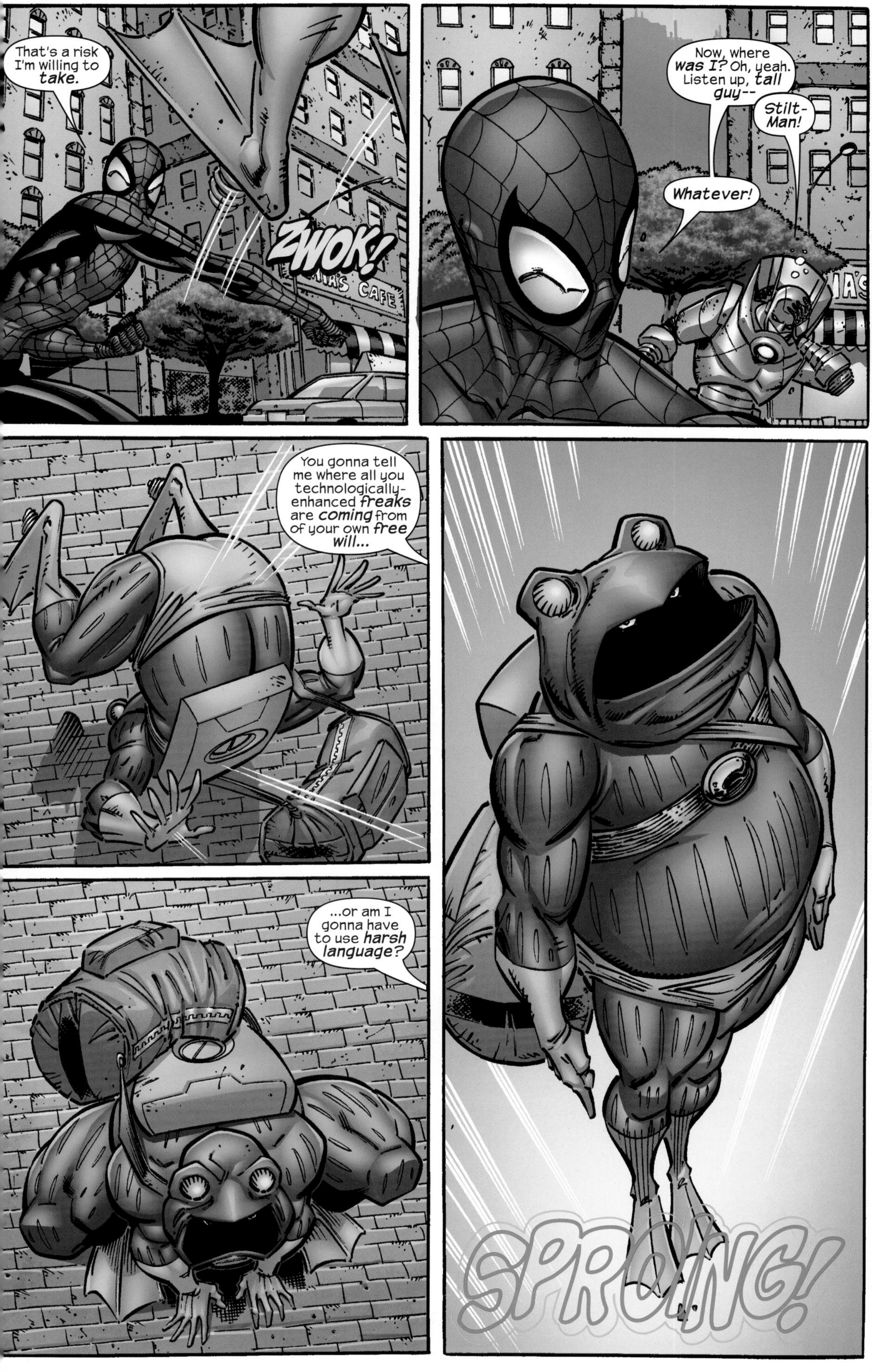
That's a risk I'm willing to take.
ZWOK!
CAFE
Now, where was I? Oh, yeah. Listen up, tall guy--
Stilt-Man!
Whatever!
You gonna tell me where all you technologically-enhanced freaks are coming from of your own free will...
...or am I gonna have to use harsh language?
SPRONG!

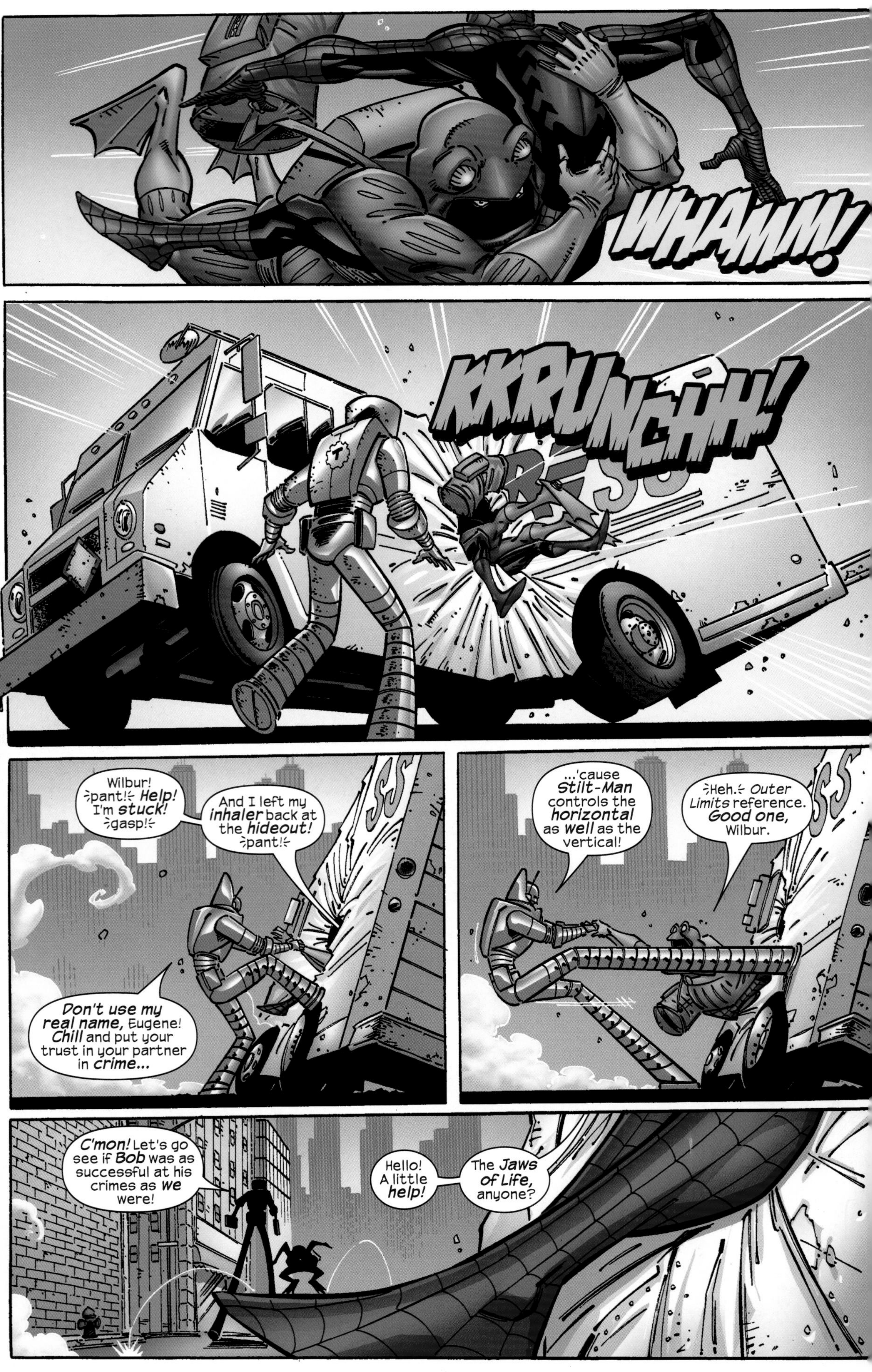
WHAMM!
KKRUNCHH!
Wilbur! pant! Help! I'm stuck! gasp!
And I left my inhaler back at the hideout! pant!
Don't use my real name, Eugene! Chill and put your trust in your partner in crime...
...'cause Stilt-Man controls the horizontal as well as the vertical!
Heh. Outer Limits reference. Good one, Wilbur.
C'mon! Let's go see if Bob was as successful at his crimes as we were!
Hello! A little help!
The Jaws of Life, anyone?

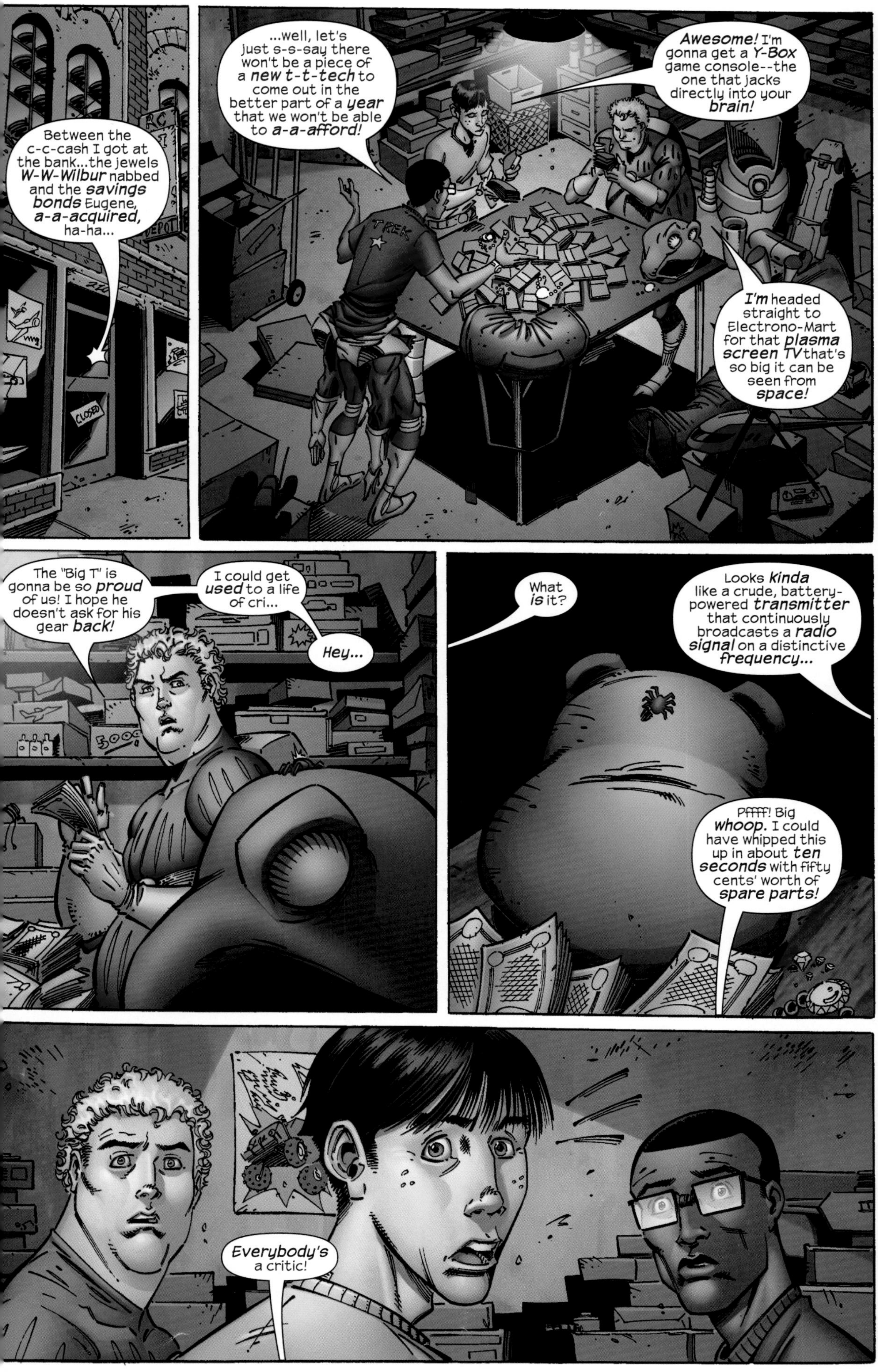
Between the c-c-cash I got at the bank...the jewels W-W-Wilbur nabbed and the savings bonds Eugene, a-a-acquired, ha-ha...
CLOSED
...well, let's just s-s-say there won't be a piece of a new t-t-tech to come out in the better part of a year that we won't be able to a-a-afford!
Awesome! I'm gonna get a Y-Box game console--the one that jacks directly into your brain!
TREK
I'm headed straight to Electrono-Mart for that plasma screen TV that's so big it can be seen from space!
The "Big T" is gonna be so proud of us! I hope he doesn't ask for his gear back!
I could get used to a life of cri...
Hey...
What is it?
Looks kinda like a crude, battery-powered transmitter that continuously broadcasts a radio signal on a distinctive frequency...
Pffff! Big whoop. I could have whipped this up in about ten seconds with fifty cents' worth of spare parts!
Everybody's a critic!

I know my *spider tracers* don't *look* like much, but they get the *job* done.

Oh *no*, you don't.

We're not going through all *that* again.

THWIP! THWIP!

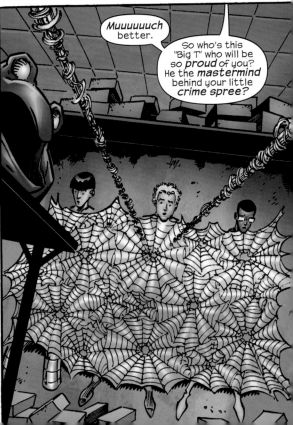

Muuuuuuch better.

So who's this "Big T" who will be so *proud* of you? He the *mastermind* behind your little *crime spree?*

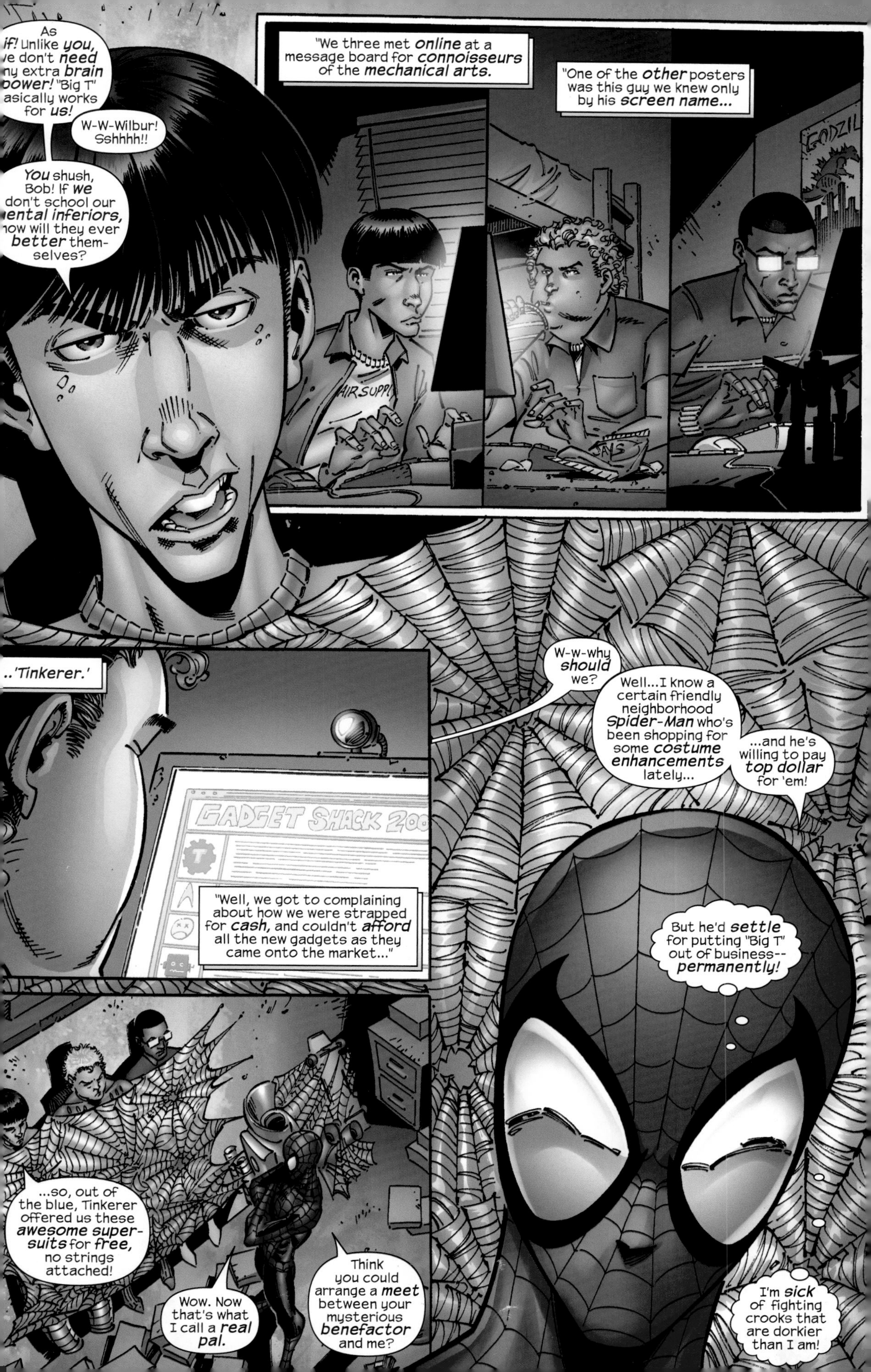
As if! Unlike you, we don't need any extra brain power! "Big T" basically works for us!
W-W-Wilbur! Sshhhh!!
You shush, Bob! If we don't school our mental inferiors, how will they ever better themselves?
"We three met online at a message board for connoisseurs of the mechanical arts.
"One of the other posters was this guy we knew only by his screen name...
...'Tinkerer.'
GADGET SHACK 200
"Well, we got to complaining about how we were strapped for cash, and couldn't afford all the new gadgets as they came onto the market..."
...so, out of the blue, Tinkerer offered us these awesome super-suits for free, no strings attached!
Wow. Now that's what I call a real pal.
Think you could arrange a meet between your mysterious benefactor and me?
W-w-why should we?
Well...I know a certain friendly neighborhood Spider-Man who's been shopping for some costume enhancements lately...
...and he's willing to pay top dollar for 'em!
But he'd settle for putting "Big T" out of business--permanently!
I'm sick of fighting crooks that are dorkier than I am!

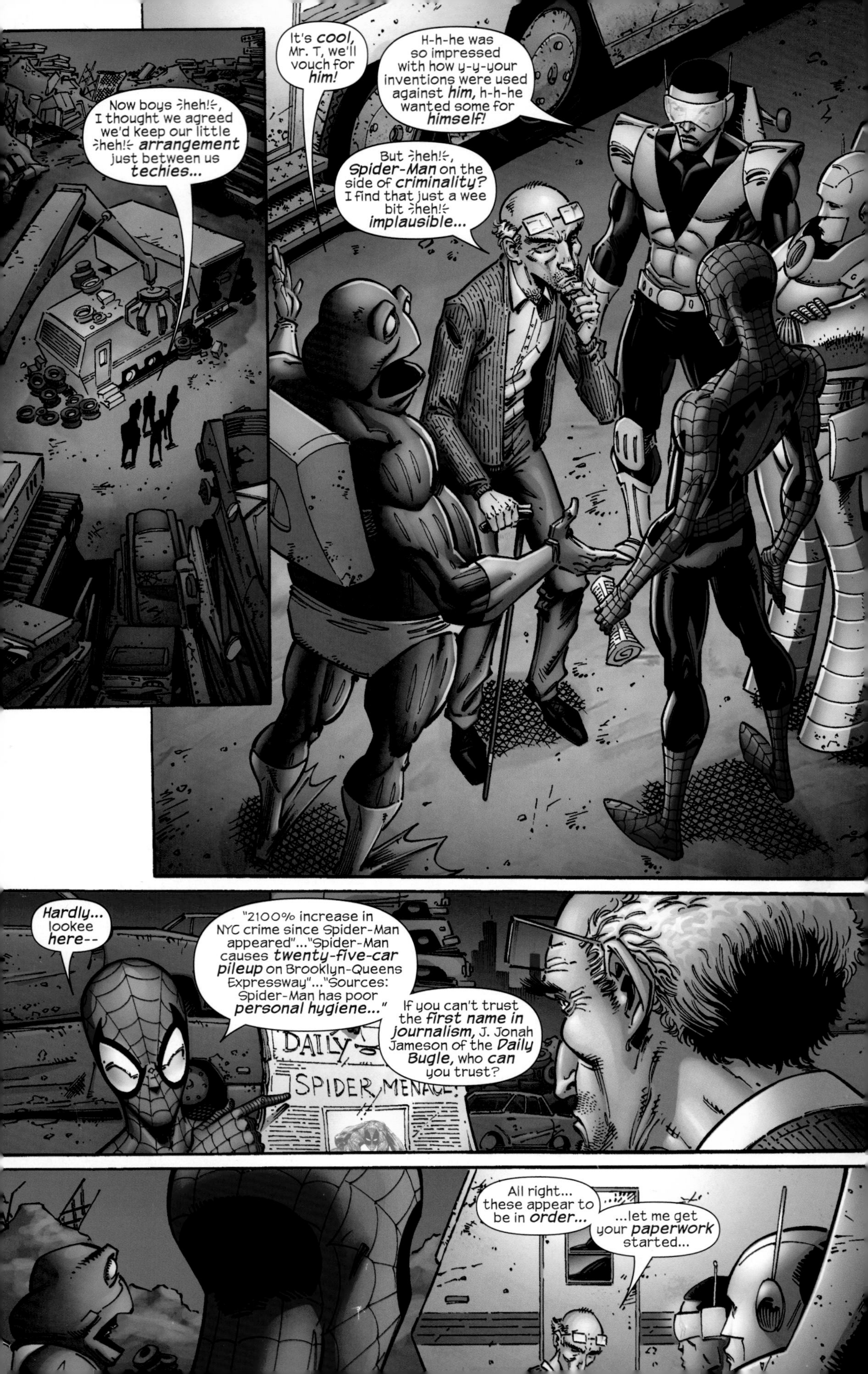
Now boys ⫘heh!⫗, I thought we agreed we'd keep our little ⫘heh!⫗ arrangement just between us techies...
It's cool, Mr. T, we'll vouch for him!
H-h-he was so impressed with how y-y-your inventions were used against him, h-h-he wanted some for himself!
But ⫘heh!⫗, Spider-Man on the side of criminality? I find that just a wee bit ⫘heh!⫗ implausible...
Hardly... lookee here--
"2100% increase in NYC crime since Spider-Man appeared"..."Spider-Man causes twenty-five-car pileup on Brooklyn-Queens Expressway"..."Sources: Spider-Man has poor personal hygiene..."
If you can't trust the first name in journalism, J. Jonah Jameson of the Daily Bugle, who can you trust?
DAILY
SPIDER MENACE!
All right... these appear to be in order...
...let me get your paperwork started...

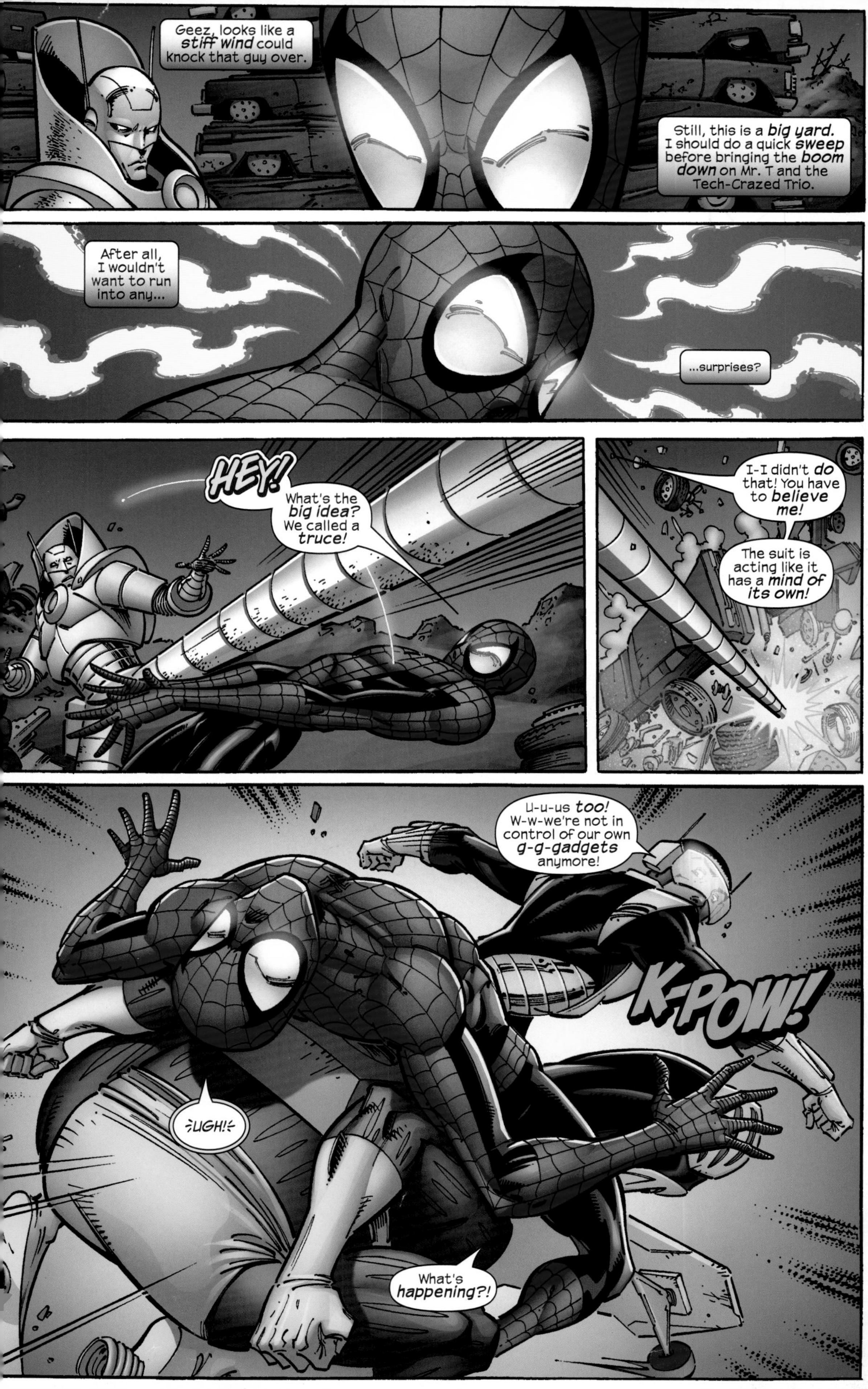
Geez, looks like a stiff wind could knock that guy over.
Still, this is a big yard. I should do a quick sweep before bringing the boom down on Mr. T and the Tech-Crazed Trio.
After all, I wouldn't want to run into any...
...surprises?
HEY!
What's the big idea? We called a truce!
I-I didn't do that! You have to believe me!
The suit is acting like it has a mind of its own!
U-u-us too! W-w-we're not in control of our own g-g-gadgets anymore!
K-POW!
UGH!
What's happening?!

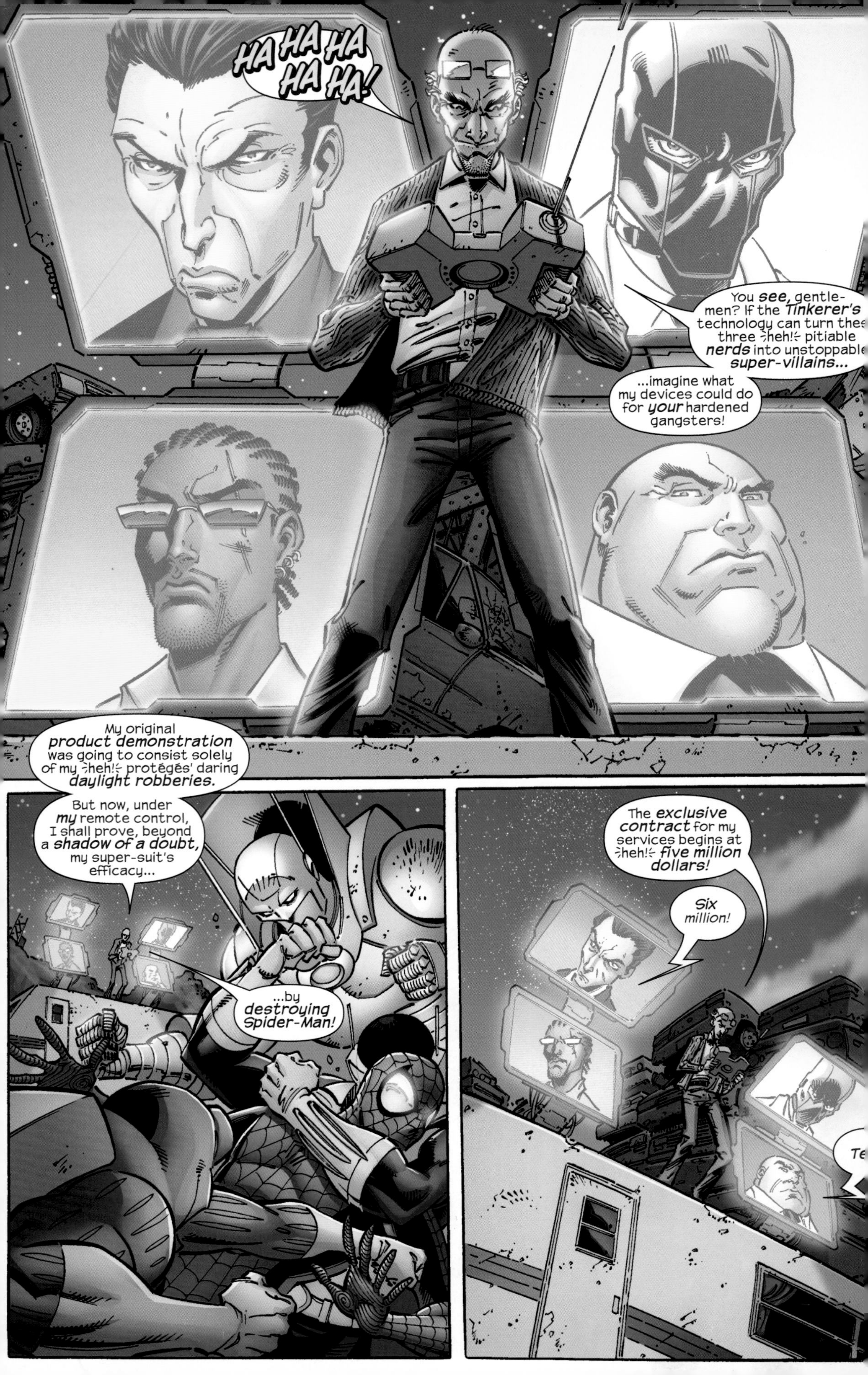
HA HA HA HA HA!
You see, gentle-men? If the Tinkerer's technology can turn thes three -heh!- pitiable nerds into unstoppabl super-villains...
...imagine what my devices could do for your hardened gangsters!
My original product demonstration was going to consist solely of my -heh!- protégés' daring daylight robberies.
But now, under my remote control, I shall prove, beyond a shadow of a doubt, my super-suit's efficacy...
...by destroying Spider-Man!
The exclusive contract for my services begins at -heh!- five million dollars!
Six million!

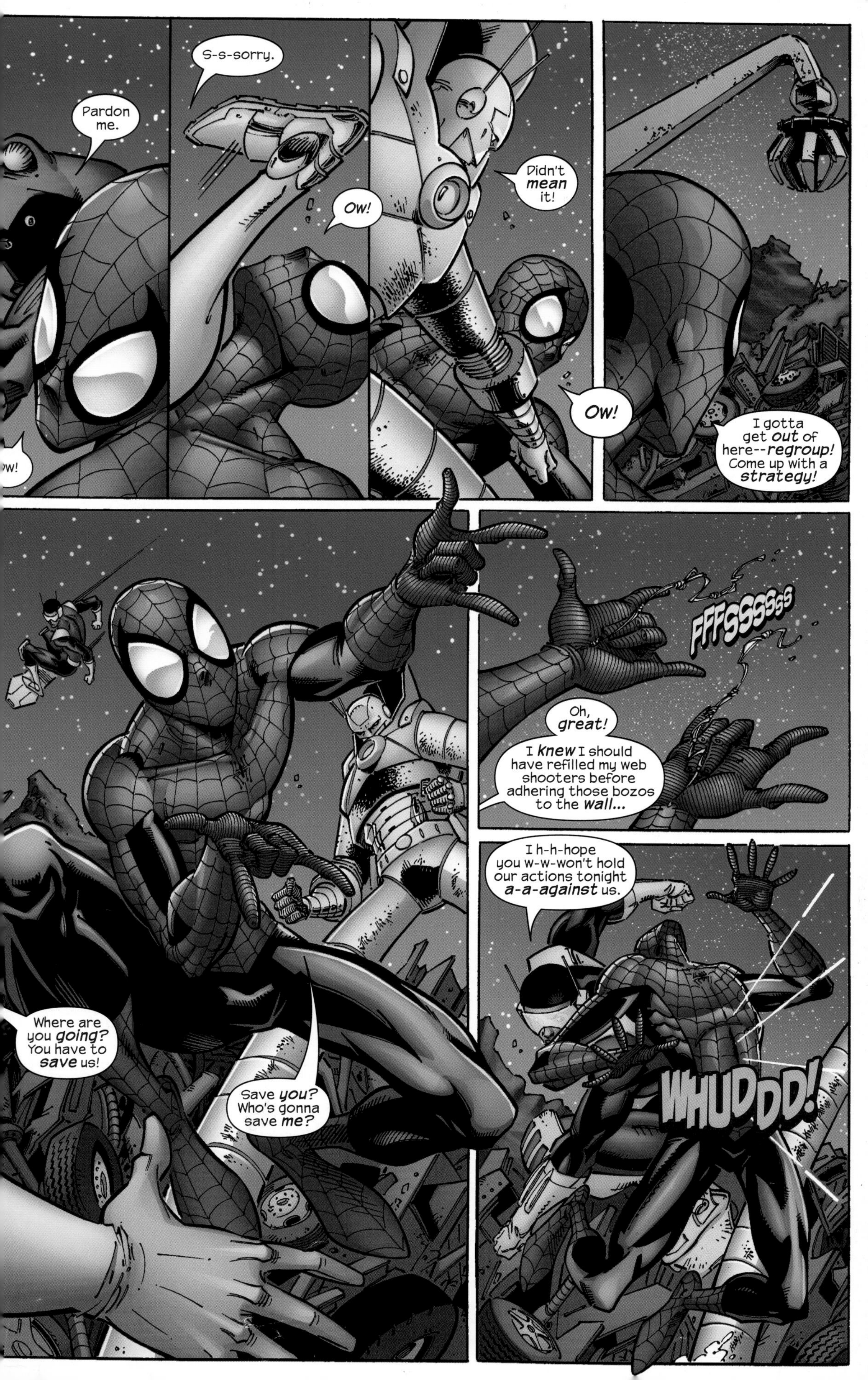
Pardon me.
OW!
S-s-sorry.
OW!
Didn't mean it!
OW!
I gotta get out of here--regroup! Come up with a strategy!
Where are you going? You have to save us!
Save you? Who's gonna save me?
FFFSSSSSS
Oh, great!
I knew I should have refilled my web shooters before adhering those bozos to the wall...
I h-h-hope you w-w-won't hold our actions tonight a-a-against us.
WHUDDD!

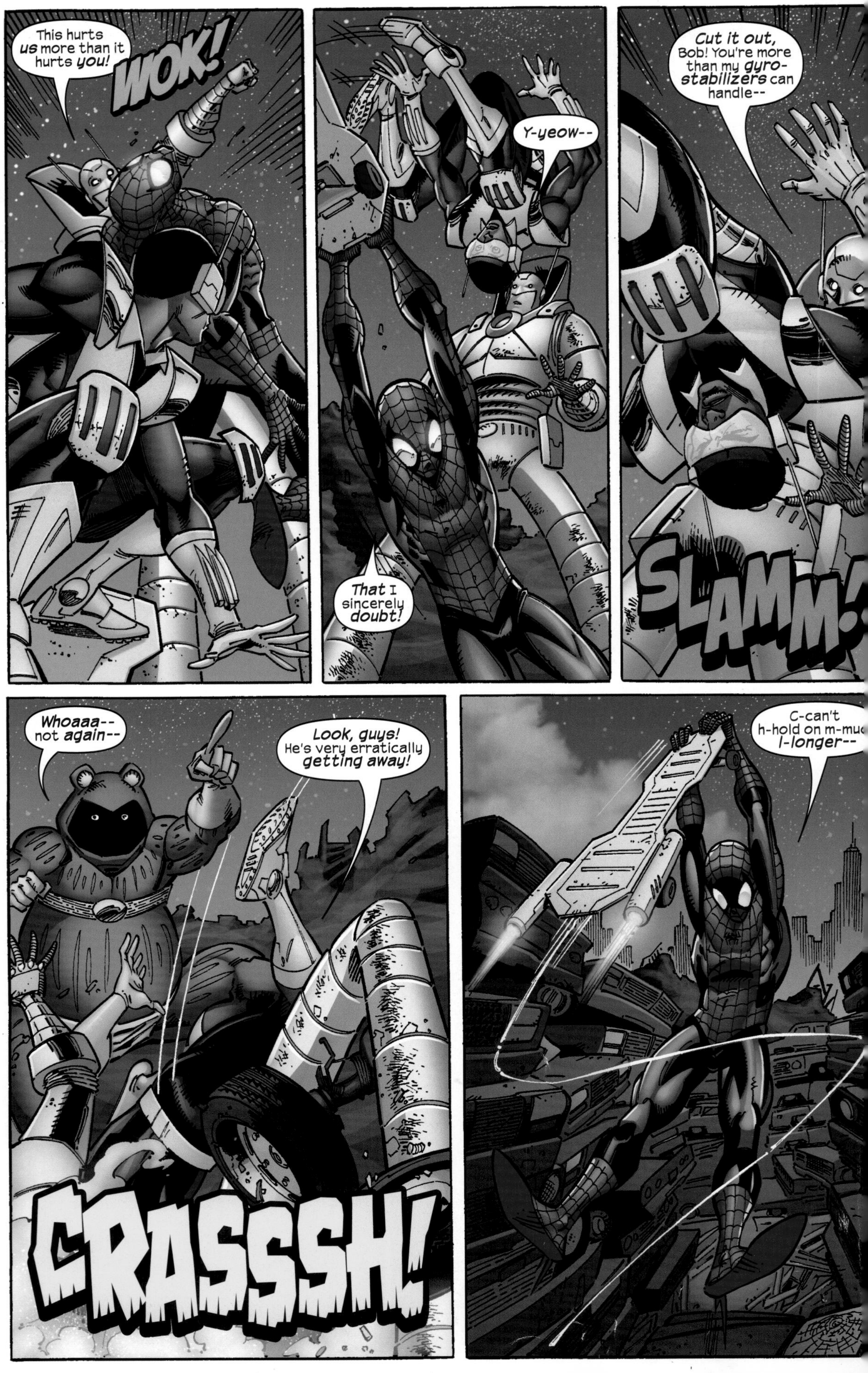
This hurts us more than it hurts you!
WOK!
Y-yeow--
That I sincerely doubt!
Cut it out, Bob! You're more than my gyro-stabilizers can handle--
SLAMM!
Whoaaa-- not again--
Look, guys! He's very erratically getting away!
CRASSSH!
C-can't h-hold on m-muc l-longer--

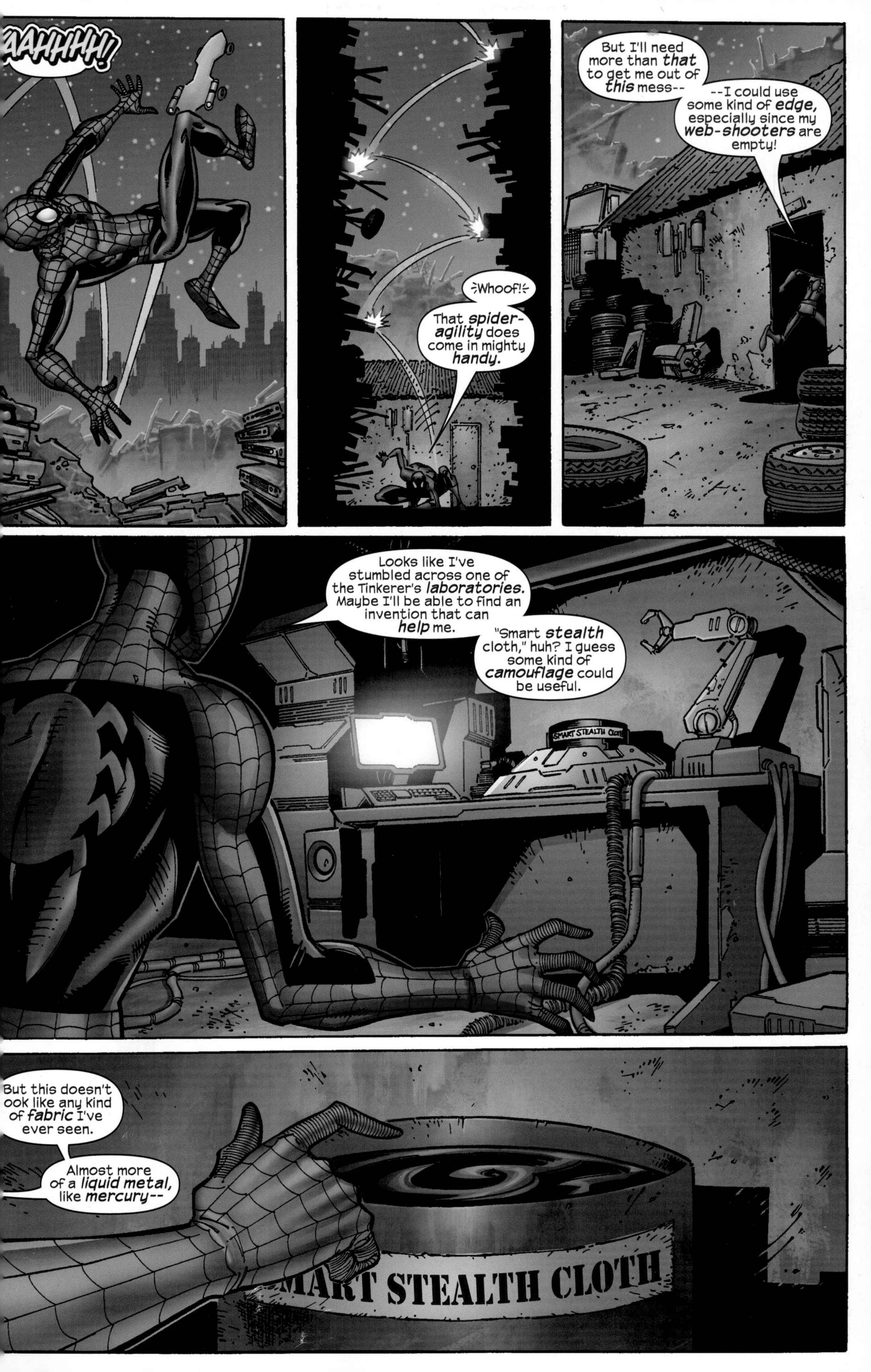
AAHHHH!
Whoof!
That spider-agility does come in mighty handy.
But I'll need more than that to get me out of this mess--
--I could use some kind of edge, especially since my web-shooters are empty!
Looks like I've stumbled across one of the Tinkerer's laboratories. Maybe I'll be able to find an invention that can help me.
"Smart stealth cloth," huh? I guess some kind of camouflage could be useful.
SMART STEALTH CLOTH
But this doesn't look like any kind of fabric I've ever seen.
Almost more of a liquid metal, like mercury--
SMART STEALTH CLOTH

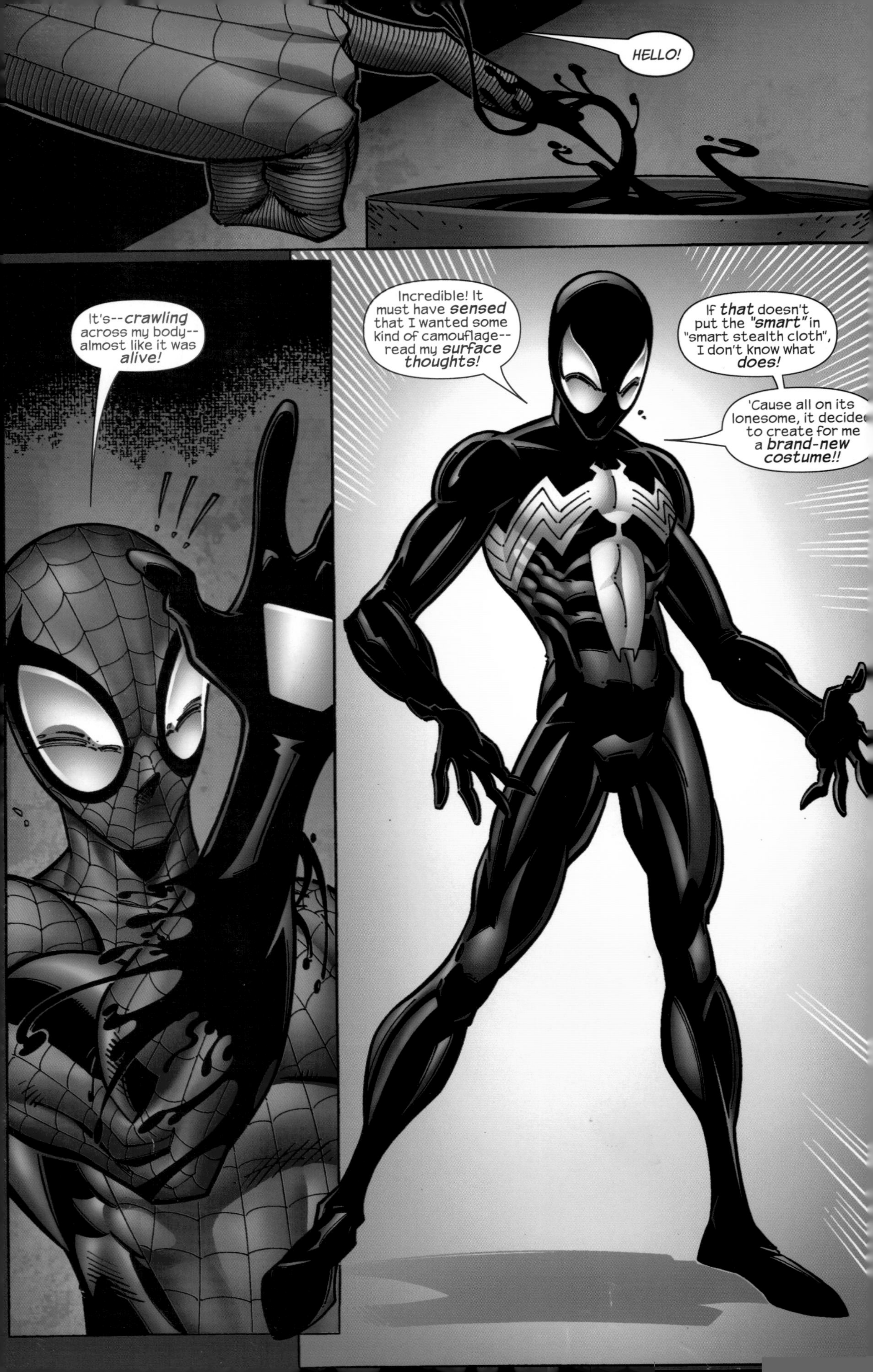
HELLO!
It's--crawling across my body--almost like it was alive!
Incredible! It must have sensed that I wanted some kind of camouflage--read my surface thoughts!
If that doesn't put the "smart" in "smart stealth cloth", I don't know what does!
'Cause all on its lonesome, it decided to create for me a brand-new costume!!

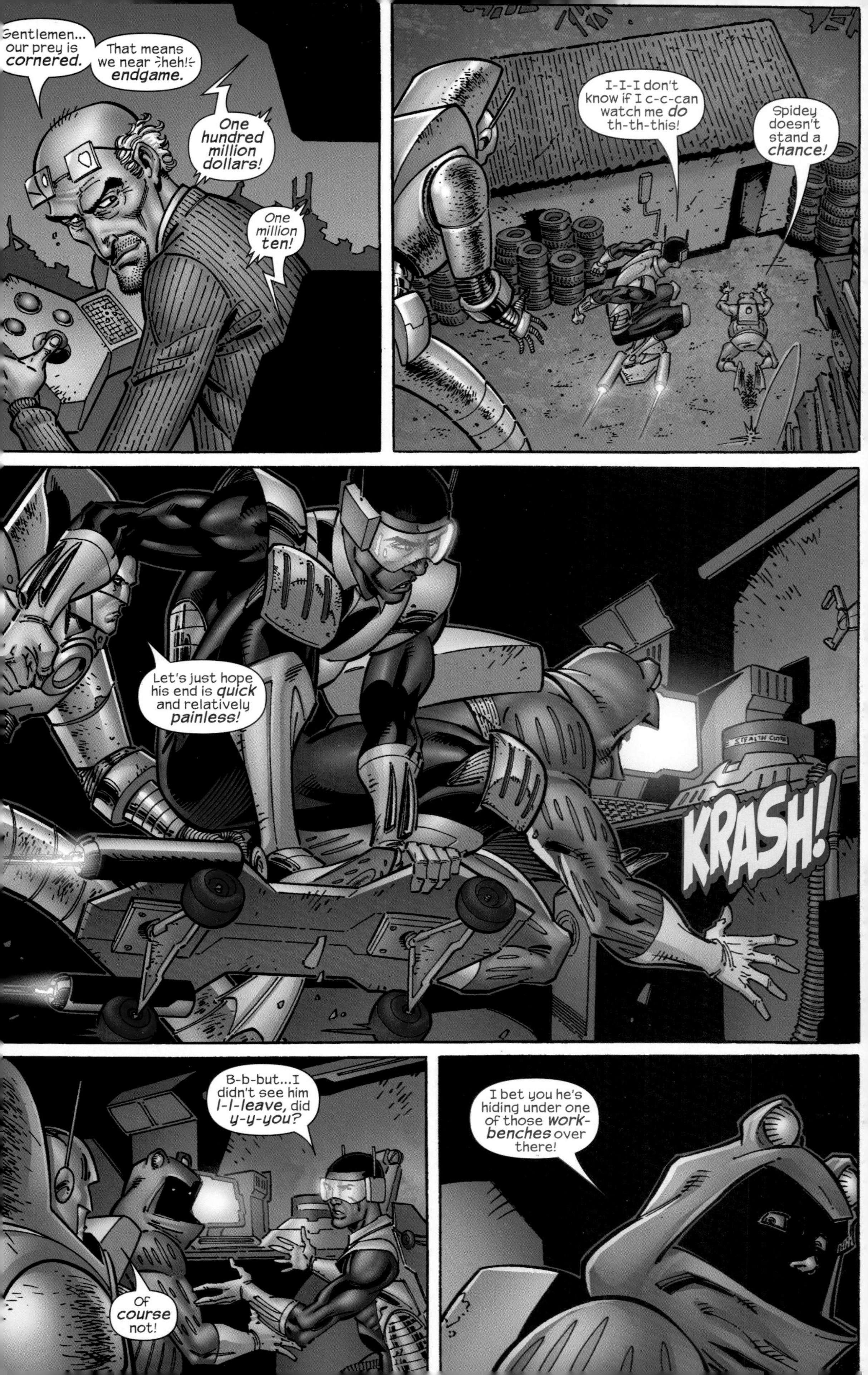
Gentlemen... our prey is cornered.
That means we near -heh!- endgame.
One hundred million dollars!
One million ten!
I-I-I don't know if I c-c-can watch me do th-th-this!
Spidey doesn't stand a chance!
Let's just hope his end is quick and relatively painless!
KRASH!
B-b-but...I didn't see him l-l-leave, did y-y-you?
Of course not!
I bet you he's hiding under one of those work-benches over there!

If it's possible to fall in *love* with a pair of *long underwear*, then I'm *head over heels.*

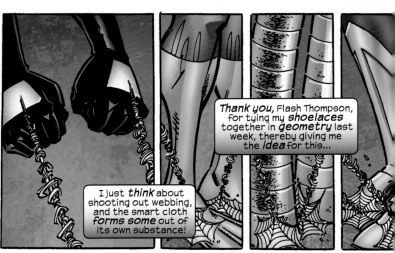

I just *think* about shooting out webbing, and the smart cloth *forms some* out of its own substance!

Thank you, Flash Thompson, for tying my *shoelaces* together in *geometry* last week, thereby giving me the *idea* for this...

Hey! *Tinkerer!*

Don't just *do* something! *Stand* there!

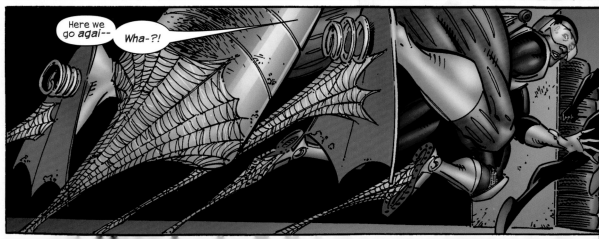

Here we go *agai--*

Wha-?!

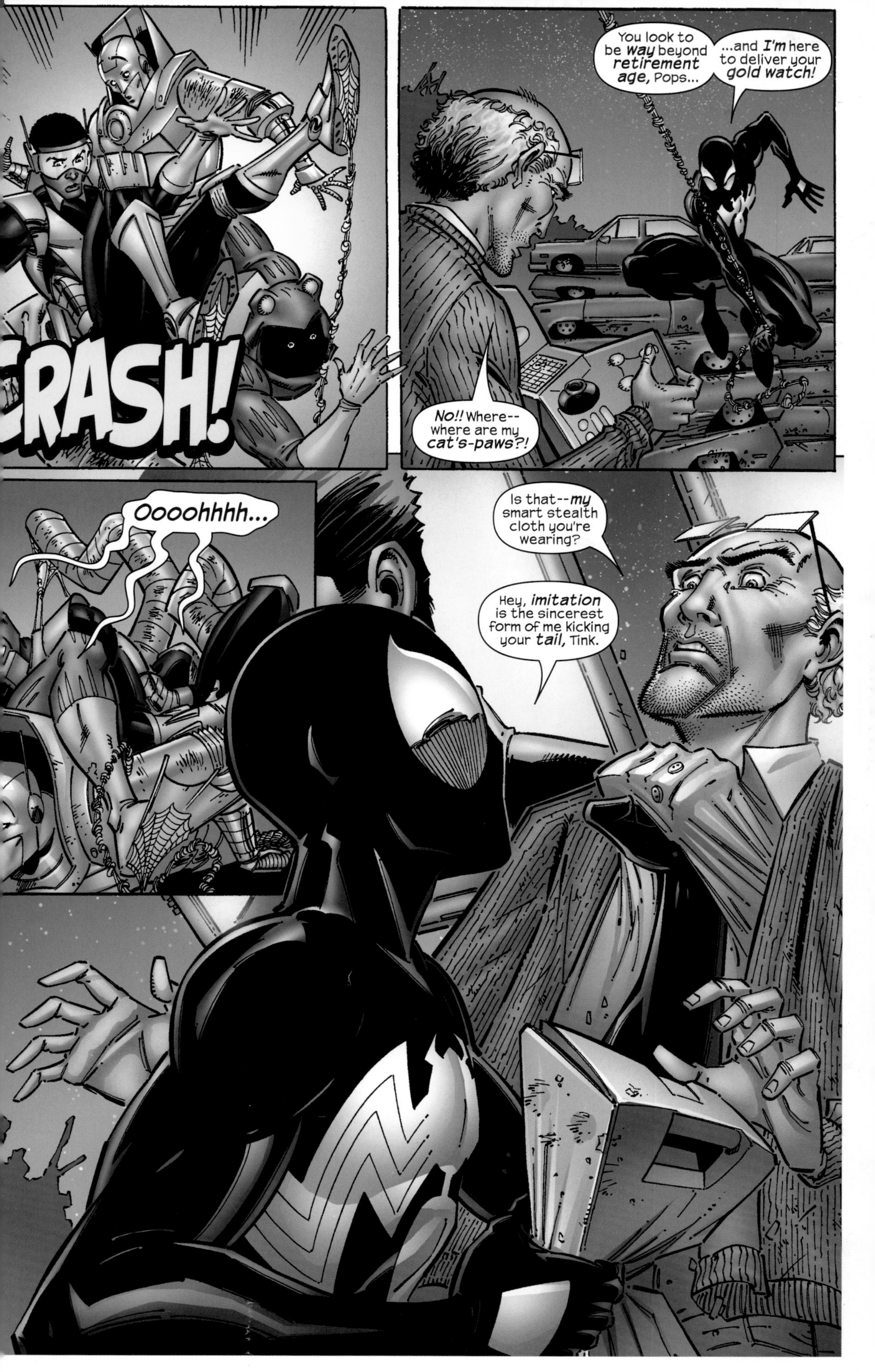
CRASH!
You look to be *way* beyond *retirement age,* Pops...
...and *I'm* here to deliver your *gold watch!*
No!! Where-- where are my *cat's-paws?!*
Oooohhhh...
Is that--*my* smart stealth cloth you're wearing?
Hey, *imitation* is the sincerest form of me kicking your *tail,* Tink.

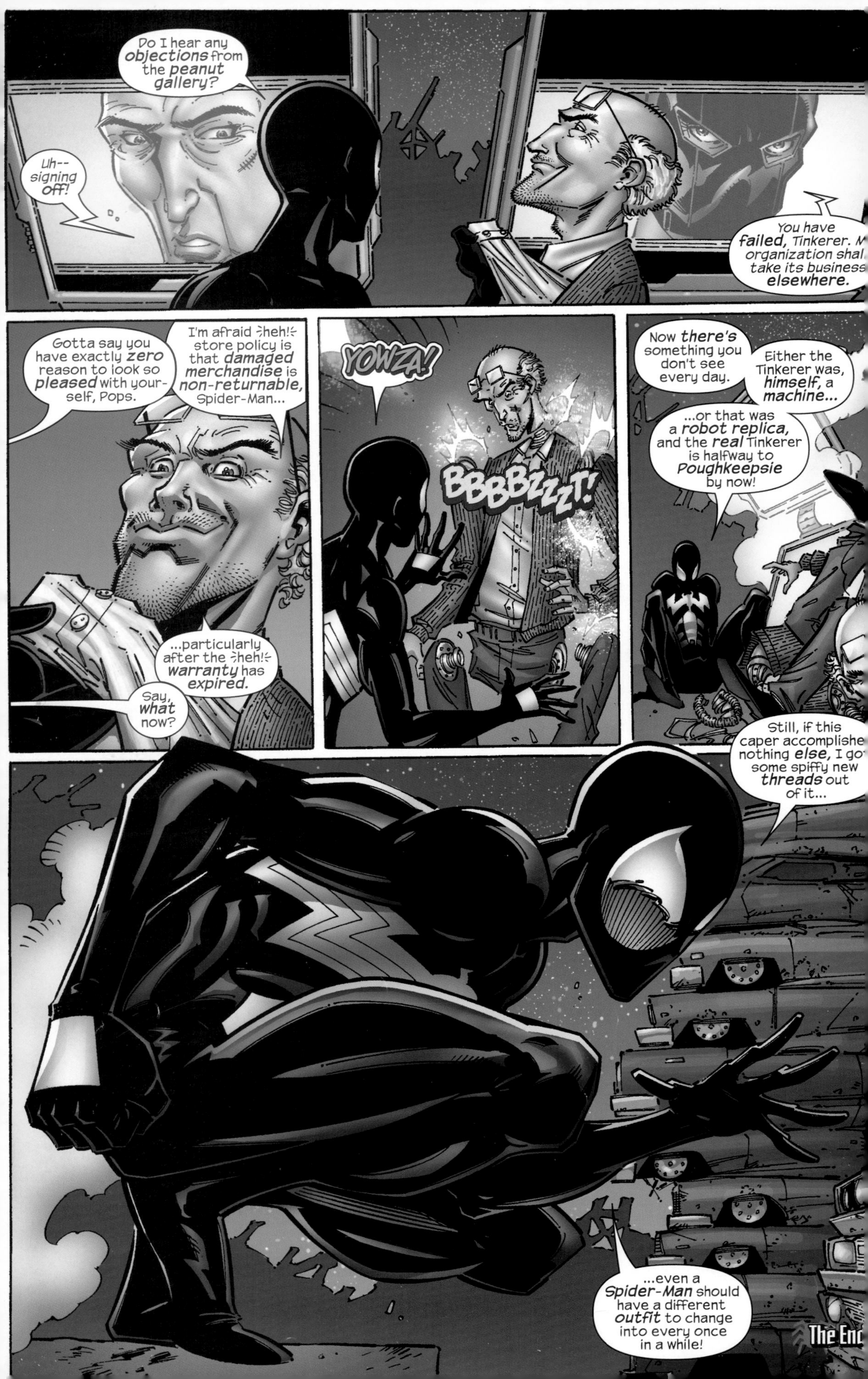

Do I hear any objections from the peanut gallery?
Uh-- signing off!
You have failed, Tinkerer. M organization shal take its business elsewhere.
Gotta say you have exactly zero reason to look so pleased with your-self, Pops.
I'm afraid -heh!- store policy is that damaged merchandise is non-returnable, Spider-Man...
...particularly after the -heh!- warranty has expired.
Say, what now?
YOWZA!
BBBBZZZT!
Now there's something you don't see every day.
Either the Tinkerer was, himself, a machine...
...or that was a robot replica, and the real Tinkerer is halfway to Poughkeepsie by now!
Still, if this caper accomplishe nothing else, I go some spiffy new threads out of it...
...even a Spider-Man should have a different outfit to change into every once in a while!
The End